"What do we do now?" Norman said, scratching his head. "You can't play ball without a third base."

"I know!" T.J. cried suddenly. "James, won't Tag stay where you tell him to?"

"Oh, no, you don't, T.J.," James said firmly. "You're not going to use my dog for third base."

"Oh, come on, James," T.J. answered impatiently. "It's not like we're going to slide into third or anything—and we'll throw the ball easy, too. We'll be careful. I promise Tag won't get hurt."

"Welllll . . ." James still wasn't sure. Tag cocked his head, a puzzled look on his face, as if he knew they were talking about him. "I guess it's okay," James decided at last. "But no rough stuff, guys. I don't want anything to happen to Tag."

"Don't worry, nothing will," T.J. promised.

But T.J. was wrong . . .

DOG ON THIRD BASE

CONSTANCE HISER

A MINSTREL® BOOK

PUBLISHED BY POCKET BOOKS

New York   London   Toronto   Sydney   Tokyo   Singapore

This book is a work of fiction. Names, characters, places, and incidents
are either products of the author's imagination or are used fictitiously. Any
resemblance to actual events or locales or persons, living or dead, is
entirely coincidental.

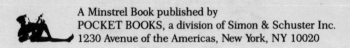
A Minstrel Book published by
POCKET BOOKS, a division of Simon & Schuster Inc.
1230 Avenue of the Americas, New York, NY 10020

Text Copyright © 1991 by Constance Hiser
Illustrations copyright © 1991 by Carolyn Ewing

Published by arrangement with Holiday House, Inc.

ISBN: 0-671-78962-7

First Minstrel Books printing March 1993

10 9 8 7 6 5 4 3 2 1

A MINSTREL BOOK and colophon are registered trademarks
of Simon & Schuster Inc.

Cover art by Tom Galasinski

Printed in the U.S.A.

For Ron,
who taught me everything I know
about baseball

C. H.

Contents

1. Foul Ball!   3
2. Home Run!   11
3. Trouble with Tiger   20
4. Tag on Third   28
5. The Search Is On   36
6. Right through the
   Window!   47
7. Who Needs Luck?   59

CHAPTER ONE

Foul Ball!

On, no! James groaned. T. J. had just hit the ball—hard. It sailed out into left field, and was falling down, down, down out of the blue sky, straight toward him. James had spent the whole game kicking up the dirt, hoping no one would hit a fly ball anywhere near him.

Now he felt a little sick to his stomach as he squinted up into the sunshine and stumbled across the grass, his glove stretched out toward the spot where he hoped the ball would come down. He could see it falling

3

closer—closer, and he heard all the kids yelling and jumping up and down. James took a deep breath and lunged for the ball. . . .

Thud! That was the sound the baseball made as it crashed to the ground right at James's feet. James winced as he looked down at it. He had come so close—that ball was practically in his glove! How could he have missed again?

Shoulders slumping, James sighed as he dragged himself toward the plate to take his turn at bat. He hated baseball. It was the one thing he never could do as well as his friends. "Why do we have to spend the whole spring break playing this dumb game anyway?" he muttered. "It's not like we couldn't ride bikes or read comic books or something."

Tag, his funny-faced, brown-and-white dog, licked his hand as he bent down to pick up his old baseball bat.

"Never mind, James," T.J. said. "Everyone misses sometimes."

"Yeah," James sighed, thumping the bat

4

on the ground and making little puffs of dust swirl in the air. "Sometimes, sure. But *every* time? I never catch that ball, T.J., and you know it. Sometimes I wonder why I ever bother to try."

T.J., Pete, Mike, and Norman traded glances. It was true—James was the worst player in the gang. He didn't do a very good job in the field, and he was even worse at bat. But they didn't talk about it much—after all, he was pretty good at football and basketball. And it was like they kept reminding him—no one could be good at *everything*.

"Don't worry about it," T.J. said, tossing her pigtails over her shoulders as she walked back out to the pitcher's mound. "Who knows—maybe this will be the day you hit a home run."

"Yeah," James mumbled, shouldering the bat, "and maybe this will be the day we find a million dollars, too—only I wouldn't count on it."

But maybe she's right, he tried to tell himself as he stepped up to the plate, gripping

5

the bat so hard his knuckles turned white. Maybe I'll actually hit the ball. Maybe I'll even hit a homer. Wouldn't that be something? He could almost hear the *crack* of the bat, and the cheers of his friends. He could almost see himself sliding into home plate. . . .

"Strike one!" shouted Norman, who was the umpire today.

"Huh?" James shook his head, trying to shake the daydreams away. It had seemed so real—he hadn't even noticed the ball streaking past.

Gritting his teeth in concentration, he glared at T.J. and waited for her pitch. And there it came. Desperately, James swung the bat—and heard it whistle through empty air.

"Strike two!" Norman shouted.

Oh, no! One more strike, and he was out—again. Not today, he promised himself. T.J.'s not going to strike me out again today.

And here was the pitch. James swung—and gasped as he actually felt bat meet ball. For one wonderful moment, his heart seemed to stop as he threw down the bat and ran toward first base. But then Norman yelled, "Foul ball!"—and, a second later, Pete groaned, "Oh, no! Look where it's going."

" 'Oh, no' is right!" Mike shouted. "It's headed straight for Mrs. Abernathy's yard!"

Now James's stomach really did hurt as he watched his foul ball plunge straight down into old Mrs. Abernathy's prize daffodil bed. Yellow petals flew everywhere, and Tag gave an excited bark as a stray cat shot up from the ground with a terrified yowl.

"Now we've had it," T.J. said in a whisper, her face white under her freckles. "Here she comes!"

Sure enough, Mrs. Abernathy's kitchen door had just crashed open, and the crabby old lady marched across her front yard toward the vacant lot.

"She doesn't look very happy," Mike said. He sounded as sick as James felt.

"Children," Mrs. Abernathy snapped as she stooped over her daffodil bed to snatch a handful of crushed flowers, "don't even think about running away. I have a few things to say to you."

Shuffling their feet in the dirt, the kids stared at their shoes, not daring to look into her angry face. "Y-yes, Mrs. Abernathy?" T.J. said in a small voice.

Mrs. Abernathy's eyes narrowed as she glared at them. "This is the last straw," she scolded. "You children have ruined some of my very best daffodils—the ones I was planning to enter in the big flower show. And it's not the first time either."

"It's my fault," James said, although he was so frightened that his tongue stuck to the roof of his mouth. "I was the one who hit the ball, Mrs. Abernathy. And I really am sorry about your flowers."

"Sorry isn't good enough!" Mrs. Abernathy yelled. She held up a couple of daffodils, their stems broken and their yellow petals torn. "Look at my poor flowers. And it was only yesterday that someone tramped through my tulip bed and squashed half of

those. I'm tired of it, I tell you." She sounded angrier and angrier with every word she spoke. "I don't know why you have to play in that lot anyway. Someone ought to do something about it. Maybe *I* will. Maybe I'll call the police."

The police! The kids suddenly stiffened and exchanged terrified looks. Mrs. Abernathy was just mean enough to do it, too.

"Please, Mrs. Abernathy," T.J. begged, "we broke your flowers today, but we didn't tramp through your tulips. We never go into your yard, except to catch a ball or something, and then we're really careful."

"Well," Mrs. Abernathy sniffed, "if you kids didn't do it, who did? I'm warning you once more—the next time I find one smashed flower—*even one*—the police are going to hear from me. That will put a stop to these silly ball games."

And, while the gang stood rooted to the ground, the old lady turned and stomped back into her house, letting the door slam behind her.

10

CHAPTER TWO

Home Run!

"I don't know about this, T.J.," Mike said uneasily when the gang met for batting practice at the vacant lot the next day. "Mrs. Abernathy's yard is just so *close*—it's impossible to keep from hitting balls over there. And you know what she said yesterday."

"Yeah." Pete shivered a little as he glanced across the vacant lot at Mrs. Abernathy's house. "I don't know what my folks would say if she really called the police. Can't we play someplace else, T.J.?"

"Where?" T.J. demanded. "You know the

ball field at the park is all torn up while they put in new bleachers. And the sixth graders always hog the playground at school. If we want to play at all, this is the only place."

"So how do we keep Mrs. Abernathy from getting mad?" James asked. "Personally, T.J., I'd just as soon we go ride our bikes or something."

"Ruff!" Tag agreed, wagging his tail.

T.J. sighed. "Oh, come on, guys! We'll just have to be extra careful not to hit the ball into those flowers, that's all. I don't like it any more than you do, but we have a big game coming up at school next week, re-member? With the fifth graders. We've got to beat them. And some of us really need the batting practice."

She didn't look at James when she said that, but he knew who it was she was talking about, all right.

The boys shook their heads and muttered under their breath as they reached for their bats and gloves. "I hope we don't get killed," Pete said, heading for center field.

"Want first bat, James?" Norman asked.

James shook his head. "I think I'll watch you guys first," he said. "Maybe I'll get some pointers."

He hung back at the edge of the lot, and let everyone else bat before he took a turn. First Norman pitched to T.J., then T.J. pitched to everyone else. And James had to admit that they were all pretty good, especially T.J., who hit the ball almost every time. He wished he didn't have to bat at all. He wished he didn't have to look so stupid in front of his friends.

"Come on, James, your turn," T.J. called.

"I think I'll skip this time," he called back. "My hand has a blister on it from holding the bat."

"It does not!" T.J. yelled. She rolled her eyes as she left the pitcher's mound. The other boys glanced at each other, then began to stroll toward T.J. As James watched, the four of them put their heads together and whispered for a few seconds.

"What's going on out there?" James

called. "Hey, what are you guys talking about?"

The little huddle near the pitcher's mound broke up, and T.J. walked over to James, followed by the boys. "Look, James," she said, "we were just thinking. Maybe it would help if you used my bat."

James looked at the bat she was holding out to him. "But I have a bat," he argued. "Why should I use yours?"

T.J. lowered her voice and leaned forward as if she were about to tell a big secret. "Because it's my *lucky bat,*" she explained. "My folks gave it to me last Christmas, and I started batting better right away."

James looked closely at the bat. It looked like his, except the stripe around the grip was red, and the stripe on his was black.

"It looks like an ordinary old baseball bat to me," he said. "Are you sure it's a lucky bat?"

"You saw T.J. just now," Pete reminded him. "This was the bat she was using, and she hit the ball almost every time."

"Yeah . . ." James looked at the bat again,

wanting to believe him. He still wasn't sure. "T.J. was always a good batter."

T.J. shrugged. "Well, I'm even better now," she pointed out. "And it's because of my lucky bat! Come on, James, won't you at least give it a try?"

"Wellllll . . ." James reached out for T.J.'s bat.

"That's the spirit!" T.J. cheered. "Look, just stand there and take your best swing, okay? It doesn't even matter if you miss a few times. How are you ever going to get any better if you don't practice?"

"Yeah," Norman added, "T.J. probably won't even hit you with a wild pitch or anything."

Great. He hadn't even *thought* of *that*. James dragged his feet all the way up to the plate, where Pete slapped him on the back and Mike gave him a thumbs-up. Easy for them, he thought, as he lifted T.J.'s bat to his shoulder and squinted into the bright sunshine, waiting for her to pitch the ball.

And here it came, an easy pitch because

T.J. was trying to be nice to him. Taking a deep breath, James braced himself, swung the bat, and—

CRAAACCCCKKKKK!

James stood openmouthed as the ball sailed up, up, up into the sky, a tiny white speck against the blue.

"Wow," Norman gasped, "look at that thing *go!*"

"You know what that *was?*" T.J. said in a funny kind of whisper. "That was a *home run!*"

James's heart pounded in his throat. "It—it *was?*" he croaked.

"Of course it was!" Mike shouted, and Pete agreed.

"See?" T.J. laughed. "I *told* you it was a lucky bat." But she looked a little surprised herself.

James sank down onto the ground. His knees were feeling weak. "I can't believe it," he said. "I hit a *home run.*"

"I knew you could!" T.J. cheered. "I knew you could do it. Here, try it again."

"I don't know," James began. But T.J. was already running after the ball. Shivering a little as she glanced toward Mrs. Abernathy's house, she pulled the ball out of a tangle of weeds.

"You've *got* to try again," she said firmly. "If you did it once, there's no reason why you can't keep doing it. Do you know, James, if you keep hitting like that, you could be the best batter on the team."

James's grin spread across his face. "Yeah," he said. "Hey, yeah! Go ahead, T.J.—throw it again."

T.J.'s next few pitches were enough to convince James that she was right—this really *was* a lucky bat. He didn't hit the ball *every* time, and he didn't hit any more of those super home runs. But he did hit it more often than he ever had before, and a few times everyone agreed it would have been a double, maybe even a triple, if they had been playing a real game.

James stared down at the bat in his hands, more excited than he had ever been. "A lucky bat," he said. "Whoever would have imagined that?"

"Just make sure you always use that bat," T.J. told him. "Don't even bother to bring the other bat tomorrow. With you batting the way you did today, there's no way we'll ever lose a game again."

James smiled as he handed the bat back to T.J. Baseball was a terrific game after all!

CHAPTER THREE

Trouble with Tiger

"You brought your bat, didn't you, T.J.?" James called, out of breath, as he ran to meet the others, who were already waiting at the vacant lot for another afternoon of batting practice. Tag, scrambling at his heels, barked a friendly greeting to the gang.

"Sure did." T.J. held it out. "You want to go first?"

"Great!" James swung the bat a few times. "Boy, I bet I'll knock that ball so far you'll never see it again."

"Well, be a little careful about that,

James," Mike said with a tiny frown. "We only have one baseball and T.J.'s bat—we can't afford to lose anything. And be careful which way you hit it, too. You know what Mrs. Abernathy said she'd do if—"

"Hiya, babies!" They jumped as a familiar voice yelled at them from the street. "What are you little kids doing, playing roll-the-ball? Or maybe jacks? No, I know—you're having a nice game of pat-a-cake."

T.J.'s face turned bright pink. "That Mean Mitchell," she said between her teeth, "he makes me so mad." Out loud, she yelled, "We happen to be having batting practice, Mitchell. And we'd like it very much if you'd go away and leave us alone!"

James groaned. Even from this far away, he could see the way Mean Mitchell's eyes squinted up into angry little slits when T.J. yelled at him. "Cool it, T.J.," he whispered, "he doesn't look very friendly."

"Yeah," Mike added nervously, "and look at his dog."

Pete sneaked a peek at the street, and his

21

face turned white as a ghost. "Oh, no!" he gasped. "Not *Tiger*! My brother told me all about Mean Mitchell's dog. He says Tiger is the meanest dog in town."

"Don't look now, guys," Norman moaned, "but here they come."

As a mad-looking Mean Mitchell and his snarling yellow dog tramped through the weeds toward the gang, Tag began to growl. Even the hair on the back of his neck stood up in angry spikes.

"No, Tag," James begged in a whisper, "that dog is big enough to chew you up and spit you out. This is no time for you to play tough."

By now Mean Mitchell had charged close enough for them to see the nasty glint in his eyes. He was clenching and unclenching his big, hard fists. By his side, his dog Tiger was growling a loud, threatening growl. He looked almost as mean and ugly as Mean Mitchell himself. Tiger was a perfect pet for the fourth-grade bully, James decided.

"Think you're pretty big, huh?" Mean

Mitchell reached out one chubby hand and pushed Mike. Mike stumbled back and just managed to keep himself from falling. His face crumpled up as he tried to hold back tears.

"Don't do that, Mitchell!" T.J. yelled. Norman and James and Pete made a circle around Mike.

"Yeah, Mitchell," Norman echoed a little shakily, "we're not bothering you. Why don't you go away and leave us alone for a change?"

Mean Mitchell laughed. "Why should I?" he said. "Why don't we play a nice game of ball together? We're friends, aren't we? Sure we are. And you can start by giving me that bat."

As he reached to twist T.J.'s bat out of James's hands, Tag rushed at him in a blur of brown-and-white fur, barking and snarling like a dog twice his size. For an awful moment, James was afraid that Tag was going to sink his teeth into the bully's ankle—and who knew what Mean Mitchell would do then? But Mean Mitchell quickly dropped the bat and took a couple of steps backward, glaring down at Tag.

"You'd better watch that mangy mutt," he snarled, "or *my* dog will have him for lunch. Right, Tiger?"

"Rrrrrrrrrrrrrrr," Tiger agreed, stalking forward with his teeth bared. Tag looked no bigger than a puppy next to Tiger, and he whined nervously as the yellow monster got closer. Both dogs kept growling louder and louder, while T.J. yelled and James pulled at Tag's collar and Mean Mitchell laughed at them all.

"I could sic Tiger on your stupid pooch, James," he bragged. "That's what I did to that dumb mutt of the Andersons', and Tiger bit his ear clean off. If Tiger got your ugly mutt, he wouldn't leave anything but a few pieces of fur."

"No way," said T.J. "Your dog could get put to sleep for doing that."

Mean Mitchell laughed again. "Not Tiger. The Andersons' dog was on the loose, so he

got what he deserved when he came into my yard."

James gasped. "Please call your dog off, Mitchell. *Please?*"

Mitchell looked happy. "Okay," he said. "This time. But don't you guys get smart with me again, or you'll wish you hadn't. Come on, Tiger. Let's get out of here and leave these little snots to their tiddledywinks. See you later, crybabies!"

He whistled to Tiger, who growled over his yellow shoulder, and the two of them strolled off down the block.

"Errrr!" Tag whimpered. Ducking his head, he sank to the ground and covered his eyes with both front paws.

When Mean Mitchell and his dog were finally out of sight, the gang collapsed on the grass, too.

"Whew," said Norman, "that was a close one."

"*Too* close," said Pete. "I thought we were all goners for sure."

Even T.J. was shaking. "He would have

done it," she croaked. "He was really going to sic that dog on Tag—and us, too. That dog could have put us all in the hospital."

"If he didn't tear us into little bitty pieces first," James agreed, an angry gleam in his eyes. "I'm telling you, guys, if Mean Mitchell ever hurt my dog—well, I'd have to do something about it, that's all. I'd make that big bully sorry he was ever born!"

CHAPTER FOUR

Tag on Third

They were all a little nervous about coming to the vacant lot for batting practice the next day. It was bad enough that Mrs. Abernathy was watching them like a hawk from her kitchen window—but now they had Mean Mitchell and his killer dog to worry about, too.

There was no sign of the bully as they swung again and again at the ball. With T.J.'s lucky bat, James found he was batting better than ever today. He was hitting the ball at least half the time now, and with each hit it traveled farther and higher.

"You'll be our secret weapon, James," T.J. encouraged him. "You and my lucky bat— nothing can stop you."

"Yeah!" James chuckled, as he swung the bat and knocked the ball for what would have been at least a triple.

"You know what, though," T.J. said suddenly, "we really ought to practice our fielding, too. James, next time you hit, go ahead and run for first. The rest of you get to your positions—let's see if we can get him out."

"There's just one problem with that," Mike called, as they all scattered for the bases. "Third base is missing."

"What?" T.J. exclaimed. "What do you mean, third base is missing? How could it be missing?"

Mike was looking through the tall weeds. "It's gone, that's all!" he yelled back. "No sign of it. Hey, I bet anything Mean Mitchell ran away with it."

They all groaned. "That sounds like him, all right," Norman agreed.

They started searching for the big burlap sack they used for third base. Mike was right—it had disappeared completely.

"Well, how do you like that," Norman said, scratching his head. "What do we do now? You can't play ball without a third base."

They looked around. There didn't seem to be anything in the vacant lot they could use for a base—not one big rock or stray piece of plastic, not even an old tin can.

"I know!" T.J. cried suddenly. "James, won't Tag stay where you tell him to?"

"Oh, no, you don't, T.J.," James said firmly. "You're not going to use my dog for third base."

"Oh, come on, James," T.J. answered impatiently. "It's not like we're going to slide into third or anything—and we'll throw the ball easy, too. We'll be careful. I promise Tag won't get hurt."

"Welllll . . ." James still wasn't sure. Tag cocked his head, a puzzled look on his face, as if he knew they were talking about him. "I guess it's okay," James decided at last. "But no rough stuff, guys. I don't want anything to happen to Tag."

"Don't worry, nothing will," T.J. promised.

James tugged on Tag's collar until he had him in just the right spot. "Stay!" he ordered sternly. Tag looked more bewildered than ever, but he stayed right there where James had put him.

"All right!" Norman grinned. "That's some dog, James. Now—play ball."

It only took a few minutes for Tag to decide that he didn't like baseball very much. Everyone tried to be careful—instead of sliding into third, they only ran up and touched the top of the dog's head. But Tag didn't seem to care for the noise and the dust and the way people kept almost running over him. As Norman touched him on the head for the third or fourth time, Tag pointed his nose toward the sky and let out a long, loud howl.

"I knew he wouldn't like it," James said.

"Come on, guys, we've got to quit this now. It wasn't a very good idea after all."

"But then what will we use for third base?" T.J. argued. "No one's hurting him, James. Just a few minutes more and then we'll quit. I promise."

Norman shouldered the bat, looking a little uneasy as T.J.'s pitch came rushing at him. He swung hard.

Crack! Pete scrambled after the ball as it flew straight toward third base—and Tag. But Pete was too slow.

"Aroooooo!" Tag howled, as the ball crashed into his ribs.

"Oh, no," James groaned, rushing to comfort his dog. "He's hurt. I knew this was going to happen."

But Tag seemed to have decided to put an end to the ball game himself. Darting forward, he grabbed the battered old baseball in his teeth. He ran with it, just as fast as he could go, toward the big open field that lay behind the vacant lot.

"Stop him!" Mike shouted. "If he loses my

ball in all those weeds, we'll never find it!"

"Tag!" James yelled, running after his dog. "Tag, come back here!"

But Tag was fed up with baseball. He kept going, wiggling under the chain-link fence and disappearing into the tall, thick weeds on the other side.

"Oh, no," Pete groaned, "we'll never catch him now."

"And he might be hurt." James stared toward the place where his dog had vanished. "What a dumb idea, using Tag for third base. I told you it wouldn't work. I told you he wouldn't like it. I told you—"

"I'm really sorry, James." Norman sounded as if he might begin to cry as he laid one hand on James's shoulder. "I didn't mean to hit him, honest. Now we have to find him."

"He didn't look like he was hurt very badly to me, the way he was running," T.J. put in. "Don't forget, though—Mean Mitchell and Tiger could be around here anywhere."

James's stomach dropped to the very bottom of his sneakers. "Oh, guys, we've just got to find him, before Mean Mitchell does!"

"Calm down, James," Pete said, "he's probably just hiding in those weeds over there. All we have to do is look."

They snagged their clothes and scratched their legs as they climbed over the fence. They called until their voices were hoarse, but there was no sign of Tag. The weeds made their skin itch, and Pete started to worry out loud about spiders and snakes. Still, they kept looking until they had searched every corner of the big field. James was almost in tears.

"Now what?" Norman wondered as they stood together at the edge of the field, pulling seeds and burrs from the legs of their jeans.

"We have to keep looking," James begged. "It's our fault Tag ran away, and our fault he's out there where Mean Mitchell can get him. I'm telling you guys, if anything happens to Tag—well, it just can't, that's all. Tag's my best friend."

CHAPTER FIVE

The Search Is On

"He must have gone back to your house, James," Mike suggested as the gang made their way out of the vacant lot. The kids wore worried expressions on their faces as they looked at James.

"I hope you know I didn't *mean* to hurt Tag," Norman said. "I like your dog."

"We wouldn't want anything to happen to him," T.J. added.

James sighed. "Yeah, I know that," he admitted. "I know you weren't trying to hurt him. Don't worry, I'm not mad anymore. I just want to find my dog. We've got to find him before Mean Mitchell and Tiger do."

"Sure we will," Norman promised, and the others all nodded. "Just tell us where you think we ought to look, and we'll get started."

James thought about it. "Mike might be right," he said. "I bet Tag would go home first thing. Why don't we start there? Then I guess there are one or two other places it wouldn't hurt to check, before—before . . ." His voice trailed off. He hated to say what he was thinking.

But Pete said it with a big sigh. "You mean, before we have to check at Mean Mitchell's house. Well, let's just hope it doesn't come to that, James. Let's hope Tag really did go home."

When they got to James's house, there was no fuzzy brown-and-white face, no happy bark. They searched everywhere—under the porch, behind the garage, in Tag's favorite napping place under the big maple tree. But it was clear that Tag had not run back home.

"Do you suppose he might be at Mrs. Abernathy's?" Mike asked uneasily as they passed the old lady's house. "Dogs like to dig in flower gardens, don't they?"

"Oh, he wouldn't go in there!" James gasped. "At least, I hope he wouldn't. I hate to think what she'd do to him if she caught him anywhere near her precious flowers."

They took a look as they went by, anyway, just in case. But there was no sign of Tag among Mrs. Abernathy's neat beds of tulips and daffodils and hyacinths.

"At least she's not in her yard," Mike whispered as they tiptoed carefully past the purple and yellow crocuses sprinkled across the grass.

"She must be baking," Pete answered, his nose twitching. "Isn't that chocolate chip cookies I smell? Mmmmmmmmmmm!"

James glared at him. "How can you even *think* of cookies at a time like this?" he demanded.

"Uh, sorry, James," Pete apologized. "Where should we look next?"

"Well, maybe Tag went to see the Selsors' rabbits," James said, as they crossed the street and headed down Maple. "They keep them in the big hutch in back of their house, remember? Sometimes Tag likes to go there, just to sniff around."

But there was no Tag in front of the big rabbit hutch, eyeing the fuzzy white rabbits.

He wasn't at the meat market begging for scraps either, or at the park chasing Frisbees, or in the Harrisons' yard, teasing their big yellow cat. In fact, he wasn't in any of the places where James had hoped he might be . . . which left just one place—and none of them wanted to go there.

"Well, I guess we're stuck with it, guys," T.J. said unhappily. "Like it or not, we're going to have to check things out at Mean Mitchell's house."

Norman groaned, and Pete and Mike looked gloomy.

"Maybe Tag's at the library," Mike suggested.

James glared at him. "What would Tag be

doing at the *library*?" he asked. "Dogs can't *read*! No, we've got to quit putting this off. It's starting to look more and more like Mean Mitchell's got my dog. And I'm not going to stand by and let him hurt Tag."

"He's right, guys," T.J. sighed, "we can't get out of this one. Let's go!"

Mean Mitchell lived way down Pine Street, clear past the grocery store and the dry cleaner's and the car wash. It was a long walk, but James found himself wishing it were a lot longer. His heart was thumping in his chest as he thought about Mean Mitchell and his big yellow dog, with his sharp teeth and evil eyes.

"My brother told me Tiger bit the postman once," Pete told them, as they trudged down the street. "And you know how big Mr. Di-Angelo is. What do you think that dog will do to *us*?"

"And I heard he almost killed Amy Ober-felter's cat," Mike added. "They had to take it to the vet and get it all stitched up. That's one mean dog, all right."

"Cut it out, guys," T.J. said crossly. "None of us really need to hear all that right now."

James was wishing desperately that he could just give up and go back home. Only the thought of Tag kept him going.

They finally reached Mean Mitchell's. The little gray house needed paint, and the yard was a mess of broken toys and overgrown grass. But James hardly noticed any of that as they got closer and closer, not talking anymore, walking on tiptoe on their sneakered feet.

"I hope Mean Mitchell's not home," Pete whispered. That was the last thing any of them said as they sneaked through the sagging wooden gate and into the yard.

Creeping around the corner of the house, they found themselves in a weed-filled, cluttered backyard. James looked around. Where in all this junk could Mean Mitchell be hiding Tag?

"See anything?" Norman muttered. "Gosh, this place is a mess."

"Looks like Mean Mitchell's desk at

school," T.J. said. "I don't see any sign of Tag, James. Do you think he could be in that old garage over there? Mean Mitchell might have him tied up."

"Maybe," James agreed. "Guess we'd better go over there and have a closer look."

"Do we have to?" Mike begged. "Couldn't you just stand here and call Tag?"

James shuddered. "That would be even worse," he pointed out. "If Mean Mitchell *is* around here someplace, he'd hear me for sure, and then where would we be? No, we'd better go over there and have a look in that garage."

Still tiptoeing, they made their way through the clutter of broken bottles and rusty tin cans and flat tires toward the tumbledown garage. "Shh!" James put a finger to his lips as they reached the little building. "If I stand on tiptoe, I can just about see through this little window. You all keep a lookout and yell if you see Mean Mitchell—or his dog."

Stretching as high as he could, James

peered through the dirty window into the dark garage. To his disappointment, there was no sign of Tag. He whistled softly, just to make sure, but after a few minutes he had to admit to himself that Tag was not in the garage.

Dropping back onto his feet, he said, "Well, I can't think of anywhere else he could be, unless Mean Mitchell's hidden him somewhere. Maybe—"

"Hey, you kids!"

T.J. screamed and the boys jumped as a man with a scruffy beard, dressed in dirty overalls, appeared from the back of the garage and stood glaring at them.

"What are you kids doing here?" the man yelled. "You got no business in other people's yards!"

It must be Mean Mitchell's dad, James realized, as the man shook his fist at them. Who else would be so mean?

"We—" James began, taking a deep breath. "We were just looking for—"

"I don't want you nosing around here!"

Mean Mitchell's dad interrupted. "Now all of you beat it, before I call the cops on you! You heard me! Scram!"

Scattering across the yard like frightened chickens, the kids took off. The gate seemed a million miles away, but finally they were all through it and running for their lives, down the street and around the corner.

When they stopped at last to catch their breath, they were shaking. "That awful man!" T.J. said, when they could speak again. "Now I know where Mean Mitchell gets it."

James heaved a heavy sigh. "I don't understand it," he said. "I just don't understand it. I was sure Tag would be at Mean Mitchell's."

"Don't worry," Norman said. "There must be lots of places we haven't looked yet. We'll find Tag, you'll see."

"I don't know." James wiped his hand across his eyes. "I don't know if I'll ever see my dog again."

His friends looked at each other, feeling

worried and a little scared. What if Tag really was gone for good?

"I'll tell you what, James," T.J. said, trying to sound cheerful, "why don't we go back to the vacant lot? That's the last place Tag was with us—he might be there right now, trying to find you. And if he's not there—well, we'll keep looking. We'll look all day if we have to."

James shrugged. "Why not?" he said wearily. "We've looked everywhere else I can think of. I guess he could be there."

The others tried not to look as discouraged as they felt. They slowly trailed their way back to the vacant lot.

CHAPTER SIX

Right through the Window!

James tried not to worry as he walked toward the vacant lot, but he couldn't help it. What if something horrible had already happened to Tag? What if Tiger really *had* gotten him? James couldn't bear to imagine it.

"Look!" The funny sound of Norman's voice made James look up. Norman's hand was shaking as he pointed toward the vacant lot.

"Oh, no!" T.J. gasped.

"What's Mean Mitchell doing here?" Mike

whispered. "And if he's here, then where's Tag?"

Ducking behind some tall bushes, the kids all watched the fourth-grade bully bend and pick up something from the weeds.

"My ball!" Mike said indignantly, "he's found my baseball."

"Shh," Pete warned, "we don't want him to hear us."

As they spied from the bushes, Mean Mitchell threw the ball, and Tiger sprang from the ground to chase after it. As the yellow dog fetched the ball for Mean Mitchell to throw again, Mike couldn't help moaning.

"Now I'm *really* angry," he said. "That blubberhead and his slobbery dog had better give back my ball!"

Mean Mitchell whipped around, and a nasty grin spread slowly across his big face. He had heard them!

"Well, look there, Tiger," he said with a laugh. "A bunch of scared little bunny rabbits hiding in the bushes. What do you think we ought to do to the bunnies, Tiger? Are you in the mood for a little rabbit hunt?"

"Rrrrrrrrrrrrrr," Tiger growled, showing every one of his sharp white teeth.

"Where's my dog, Mitchell?" James called, stepping out of the bushes and hoping he looked braver than he felt. The rest of the gang stepped out next to him.

"Yeah!" said Mike. "And what are you doing with that ball? It's mine!"

Mean Mitchell sneered. "Oh, yeah? Well, who cares about that dumb mutt of yours, James? And if you want your ball, Mike, why don't you come over here and get it?"

As the gang watched unhappily from the edge of the lot, Mean Mitchell picked up T.J.'s baseball bat from the grass, tossed Mike's baseball up into the air, and hit it with a *crack* that echoed like thunder.

The kids all gasped.

"Oh, no," Norman yelled, "look where it's going!"

James felt sick as he followed Norman's pointing finger. The ball was curving down, down, down, over Mrs. Abernathy's fence and straight toward her kitchen window.

"Quick," James said, "we'd better hide. If she sees us here, she'll blame us for sure."

"Chickens!" Mean Mitchell laughed, as the other kids scuttled back into the bushes.

A second later there was an earsplitting *crash* as Mrs. Abernathy's window shattered into a million pieces. Then there was a horrible silence, and all the kids, even Mean Mitchell, stared openmouthed at what he had done.

The silence didn't last for long. A few seconds later, Mrs. Abernathy's back door flew open.

Forgetting his fright, James sprang to his feet. "Tag!" he yelled, as a furry brown-and-white shape ran out through the kitchen door, straight toward him. "It's Tag. He was in Mrs. Abernathy's house."

Sure enough, Tag was wiggling on the

ground at his feet, with the baseball in his mouth. James was so happy to see him, he fell to his knees beside the dog. Tag covered his face with sloppy, wet kisses.

"Uh-oh," T.J. muttered, "here comes trouble."

Mrs. Abernathy had appeared and was marching across her yard, her eyes snapping and her face red with anger.

"You," she shouted, pointing at Mean Mitchell, "get yourself over here! Right now!"

Mean Mitchell's eyes grew wide as he glanced about nervously. To the kids' amazement; he turned and began to run away from the angry old lady.

But Tiger had caught sight of Tag, and, growling fiercely, he leaped on him, while the kids yelled.

"No!" Mean Mitchell called. His voice actually sounded *scared*. "Come back, Tiger. We have to get out of here."

He made a dive for his dog and just

managed to catch him by his collar, only inches from Tag's ear. "Let's *go!*" he yelled, pulling at the stubborn dog.

He was so busy trying to drag Tiger away that he didn't see what the rest of the kids saw. Mrs. Abernathy had come very quietly across her yard, and now she was right behind Mean Mitchell.

The bully gave a funny little squeak as the old lady reached out and grabbed the back of his shirt.

"What's the idea?" she demanded, giving him a little shake. "Trying to run away, were you? Well, I'll teach you to break my window!"

"I didn't break your window," Mean Mitchell whined, trying to twist loose. "It was *him*." He pointed to James.

"Is that so, young man?" Mrs. Abernathy snapped. She glanced at James, then back at Mean Mitchell. "Then why are *you* holding the baseball bat?"

James chuckled as Mrs. Abernathy marched Mean Mitchell back toward her house. He couldn't help it. Mean Mitchell looked so funny, squirming and struggling like that. They could hear every word as Mrs. Abernathy continued her scolding.

"You're that Mitchell boy I used to baby-sit, aren't you?" she was saying. "The one who used to eat all the toilet paper right off the roll. Now, we're going inside, and you're going to give me your phone number and address, so I can have a nice little talk with your father. Then you'll either pay for my window, or you'll work in my yard until it's paid for. Oh, yes, now that I think about it, there's a lot you could do around here. My garage needs cleaning, and the hedges need a good trimming, and of course the grass has to be cut every week. Then there's the weeding and the raking and the—"

The kitchen door slammed behind the two of them, cutting off the sound of Mean Mitchell's whining and Mrs. Abernathy's scolding.

The kids looked at each other.

"*Toilet paper?*" T. J. giggled. "Did she

really say he used to eat *toilet paper*? Can you *believe* it?"

James shook his head. "I never would have believed any of it if I hadn't seen it with my own eyes," he agreed. "But the best part is, I got Tag back!" He reached down to pat his dog's fuzzy head.

"I wonder what he was doing in Mrs. Abernathy's house?" Norman asked, looking puzzled. "How did he get in there in the first place? I wouldn't think Mrs. Abernathy was the type to like animals."

"Hey, yeah!" Pete agreed.

Mike shook his head. "What a mystery!"

Just then Mrs. Abernathy's door opened, and Mean Mitchell burst out and shuffled down the sidewalk, with Tiger at his heels. Mean Mitchell's head was down, and his fists were jammed into his pockets. The kids had never seen him look so shook up.

"I wonder what she did to him!" T.J. exclaimed, her eyes wide.

A moment later Mrs. Abernathy herself appeared in her doorway. "Children!" she shouted, when she caught sight of them standing there. "I think this belongs to you," she said, handing James the bat. "Now you get yourselves home before I call the police, you hear?"

"B-but, Mrs. Abernathy"—James hadn't even known he was planning to answer the old lady until the words were already out of his mouth—"What was my dog doing in your house?"

She gazed at Tag. "Oh, is that your dog? I thought he was a stray." She still sounded cranky. "Should have known. It's clear you don't feed him properly. I was baking cookies this morning, and I guess he smelled them, because when I opened the kitchen door, in he walked, proud as you please, as if he owned the place. He just came in and made himself at home, and he's been in my kitchen gobbling down cookies ever since."

James remembered the smell of chocolate they had noticed coming from Mrs. Abernathy's kitchen earlier that day. "He'd do that, all right," he agreed. "Tag loves chocolate chip cookies. I'm sorry he bothered you, Mrs. Abernathy."

"Oh," Mrs. Abernathy sniffed, "he wasn't all that bad. I kind of like dogs—at least they're better company than some *people* I know." She glared at the kids. "Well, what are you waiting for? Take your cookie-hogging dog and go on home, all of you!"

But James stood there for a second, looking up at the grouchy old lady. "You know," he said, "my cousin's dog just had puppies, and they all need homes. If you really like dogs, maybe you could have one of them."

"Oh, you think so, do you!" Mrs. Abernathy snapped, but she looked more surprised than angry. "And have it eat me out of house and home, I suppose! Well, I'll have to think about that. I'll have to think about it a lot."

"But, Mrs. Abernathy," James said, while the others shuffled their feet nervously behind him, "I could show you where my cousin lives. I bet they'd let you have first pick!"

"I said I'd think about it," Mrs. Abernathy said crossly.

"Yes, ma'am." James turned to follow the rest of the gang, who had started to walk toward the gate.

"Wait a minute!" James whirled around as he heard the old lady's cranky voice behind him. "I suppose if you want to come back tomorrow we can talk about it. Now go away and leave me alone."

James smiled. "Yes, ma'am, Mrs. Abernathy," he answered politely and raced after his friends.

"And don't step on my crocuses!" Mrs. Abernathy shouted after them as they made their way down the sidewalk.

They were all grinning by the time they got to the street. Even Tag gave a happy bark—the bark of a dog who's stuffed completely full of delicious chocolate chip cookies. His tail wagged back and forth, back and forth, as the kids hurried toward James's house for a snack of their own.

CHAPTER SEVEN

Who Needs Luck?

"We'd better stop and get my ball and our gloves," Mike reminded them, as they ran past the vacant lot.

"And look!" Norman exclaimed, as they retrieved their equipment. "Here's our third base. I wonder where it came from? Maybe Mean Mitchell *did* take it."

"It doesn't matter now. Let's just take it with us," T.J. suggested. "That way we'll know where it is next time we want to play."

James and his friends hurried home with Tag. The first thing James did was to fill

Tag's bowls with dog food and fresh, cool water. Then everyone grabbed a handful of cookies from the cookie jar, and headed upstairs for James's room.

"I can't believe we really found Tag!" James exclaimed, flopping down on his bed. "I was so sure Mean Mitchell and Tiger had gotten him." He sat up. "You know, we never did finish our batting practice. What do you say we go practice first thing tomorrow?"

"I don't know," Pete said nervously. "Do you think Mrs. Abernathy would mind?"

James shook his head. "Naaah—she's not so bad. Nobody who likes dogs is all that terrible." He grinned. "Besides, I was just starting to get pretty good with that lucky bat of yours, T.J."

No one answered. Instead, James saw his friends look at each other with very strange expressions on their faces.

"Well," James demanded, "what's so funny? Let me in on the joke."

"Uh . . ." T.J. fidgeted. "Uh, James, I don't exactly know how to tell you this, but that isn't a lucky baseball bat. I don't think there even *is* such a thing."

"What are you talking about?" James asked impatiently. "Of course it's a lucky bat. I never could hit the ball before, and you all saw how I hit it today. In fact, I've been hitting better ever since you let me use your bat."

"Only because you *thought* it was lucky," T.J. explained patiently. "Oh, James, don't you see? You used to stand up there and *know* you couldn't hit the ball—so you never could. So—well, I guess we all thought it might give you a little confidence if you thought it was a lucky bat, that's all."

Norman was nodding. "She's telling the truth, James," he said. "We were all in on it."

"See?" T.J. held out her baseball bat. "I didn't even bring the same bat today—I was in a hurry, and I didn't notice that I was grabbing my old bat. The 'lucky' bat had a red stripe around it, remember? This one's plain."

"What a dirty trick," James said, feeling a

61

little angry. "I can't believe all of you would do something like that to me."

"Why not? It worked, didn't it?" T.J. pointed out.

James thought about it, and his anger faded. "Yeah," he admitted, "I guess it did." Suddenly he felt dizzy. "But that means—that means . . ."

"That means you did all that terrific hitting with an ordinary bat." T.J. laughed. "Oh, James, don't you understand? You *can* play baseball after all!"

James was starting to catch her excitement. "Does that mean I don't have to play outfield anymore?" he asked.

His friends looked at each other again.

"Who knows?" Pete said at last. "You learned to bat, maybe you can learn to catch, too!"

"*Maybe*," T.J. warned, but she was grinning.

Just then Tag dragged into the room. All those chocolate chip cookies seemed to be catching up to him. As Tag lay on his back,

his full belly sticking up, James thought he had never been so happy.

"But no more cookies for you, Tag," he told the dog. "Not tonight, anyway."

"And that's not all," T.J. added, patting Tag's head. "We promise we'll never make you play baseball again—at least, not third base!"

"Aroooooo," Tag howled lazily. Then, resting his head on James's foot, he fell happily asleep.

About the Author and Illustrator

CATCH UP WITH
JAMES AND HIS FRIENDS!

❖ ❖ ❖ ❖ ❖ ❖ ❖ ❖ ❖ ❖ ❖

☐ NO BEAN SPROUTS, PLEASE!

☐ GHOSTS IN FOURTH GRADE

☐ DOG ON THIRD BASE

And Don't Miss...
CRITTER SISTERS
(Coming in Fall 1993)

By Constance Hiser

Available from Minstrel ® Books
Published by Pocket Books

701

MEET THE NEWEST DETECTIVE ON THE BLOCK!

Meet Mr. Pin, a rock hopper penguin who can't stay out of trouble. With a taste for chocolate and a nose for clues, Mr. Pin and his sidekick Maggie tackle Chicago's toughest crime cases.

Mr. Pin: The Chocolate Files

and

The Mysterious Cases of Mr. Pin

by
MARY ELISE MONSELL

Available from Minstrel® Books
Published by Pocket Books

Make Tracks for these Archway and Minstrel® titles!

Read these exciting adventures from Minstrel® Books:

Monica and Dee Ellen have pledged their
friendship in ketchup instead of in blood!
Together they solve mysteries in
The Ketchup Sisters by Judith Hollands

•

Ernie learns *How to Survive Third Grade* with
the help of a new friend. By Laurie Lawlor

•

All Bertine wanted was a bear. But suddenly
she had ten walking, talking Teddies that
sprouted from *The Teddy Bear Tree.*
By Barbara Dillon

•

Liza's in trouble before class even begins! She
thinks *Third Grade is Terrible*. By Barbara Baker

•

Who has the cooties in second grade?
Itchy Richard, by Jamie Gilson

•

Meet Mr. Pin, the penguin detective who
can't stay out of trouble: *The Mysterious Cases
of Mr. Pin* and *Mr. Pin: The Chocolate Files,*
by Mary Elise Monsell

These titles and many more fun books are available from

Published by Pocket Books

JAMIE GILSON KEEPS YOU LAUGHING!

____ **HOBIE HANSON, YOU'RE WEIRD** 73752-X/$2.95
Who said being weird isn't any fun? Hobie Hanson doesn't think so.

____ **DO BANANAS CHEW GUM?** 70926-7/$2.99
It's not a riddle, it's a test. And since Sam can't read, it's not as easy as it looks!

____ **THIRTEEN WAYS TO SINK A SUB** 72958-6/$2.99
Substitute teachers are fair game–and the boys and girls of Room 4B can't wait to play!

____ **4B GOES WILD** 68063-3/$2.95
The hilarious sequel to THIRTEEN WAYS TO SINK A SUB–Room 4B goes into the woods at Camp Trotter and has a wild time!

____ **HARVEY THE BEER CAN KING** 67423-4/$2.50
Harvey calls himself the Beer Can King, and why not? He's the proud owner of 800 choice cans. A collection his dad would love to throw in the trash!

____ **HELLO, MY NAME IS SCRAMBLED EGGS** 74104-7/$2.99
Making new friends should always be this much fun.

____ **CAN'T CATCH ME, I'M THE GINGERBREAD MAN**
69160-0/$2.75 Mitch was a hotshot hockey player, a health food nut and a heavy favorite to win the National bake-a-thon!

____ **DOUBLE DOG DARE** 67898-1/$2.75
Hobie has got to take a risk to prove he is special, too!

____ **HOBIE HANSON, GREATEST HERO OF THE MALL** 70646-2/$2.95
Hobie is determined to be a hero—even if he's over his head in trouble!

____ **DIAL LEROI RUPERT, DJ** 70252-1/$2.75

____ **HOBIE HANSON IN STICKS AND STONES AND SKELETON BONES** 74939-0/$2.99

____ **ITCHY RICHARD** 79245-8/$2.99
Who has the cooties in second grade?

Simon & Schuster Mail Order Dept. GIL
200 Old Tappan Rd., Old Tappan, N.J. 07675

Please send me the books I have checked above. I am enclosing $_____ (please add 75¢ to cover postage and handling for each order. Please add appropriate local sales tax). Send check or money order–no cash or C.O.D.'s please. Allow up to six weeks for delivery. For purchases over $10.00 you may use VISA: card number, expiration date and customer signature must be included.

Name _____

Address _____

City _____ State/Zip _____

VISA Card No. _____ Exp. Date _____

Signature _____ 373JD-17

Let

Bruce Coville

take you to the **Magic Shop**–
where adventure begins!

THE MONSTER'S RING

illustrated by Katherine Coville

JEREMY THATCHER,
DRAGON HATCHER

illustrated by Gary A. Lippincott